An I Can Read Book®

Wizard and Wart at SEA

story by Janice Lee Smith
pictures by Paul Meisel

HarperTrophy
A Division of HarperCollins*Publishers*

To William Christopher Martin
and his grandma Liz,
who taught him to love books
—J.L.S.

For Grandma Hortense
—P.M.

HarperCollins®, ®, and I Can Read Book® are trademarks of HarperCollins Publishers Inc.

Wizard and Wart at Sea

Library of Congress Cataloging-in-Publication Data
Smith, Janice Lee, date.
Wizard and Wart at sea / story by Janice Lee Smith ; pictures by Paul Meisel.
p. cm. — (An I can read book)
Sequel to: Wizard and Wart
Summary: While trying to relax on the beach with his dog Wart, Wizard uses his magic to get rid of pesky seagulls but finds his solution to be just as bad as the original problem.
ISBN 0-06-024754-1. — ISBN 0-06-024755-X (lib. bdg.)
ISBN 0-06-444218-7 (pbk.)
[1. Wizards—Fiction. 2. Magic—Fiction. 3. Animals—Fiction 4. Beaches—Fiction.]
I. Meisel, Paul, ill. II. Title. III. Series.
PZ7.S6499Wi 1995 94-3200
[E]—dc20 CIP
AC

Typography by Alicia Mikles
❖
First Harper Trophy edition, 1996.

Contents

Chapter One

"Wizard work is hard work,"
Wizard told Wart.
"Wart work is even harder,"
said Wart.
"We need a vacation,"
said Wizard.

“Let’s go to the sea
where it is nice and quiet.
We can eat and read on the beach,”
said Wizard.
“I will eat on the beach and
tan my tummy,” said Wart.

“We’re on our way!” said Wizard.

He hocused and pocused.

Poof!

Wizard and Wart were
at a hotel on the beach.
"The hotel is full," said the clerk.
"Everyone is having meetings.
There is a meeting of plumbers.
There is a meeting of pansy potters.
There is a meeting of pickle packers."
"We are a meeting
of Wizard and Wart,"
Wizard said.
"Then you may have a room,"
said the clerk.

The beach was full of pansy potters, pickle packers, and plumbers.

"This is the life," Wizard said.
"Nothing to do but read."
"And nothing to do but eat,"
said Wart.

Soon Wart fell asleep

and started to snore.

Soon Wizard was snoring too.

Suddenly Wizard heard a scream.

“Help!” yelled Wart.

Seagulls swooped around him.

“Do magic,” cried Wart.

“Make them go away!”

“I don’t work on vacation,”

said Wizard.

He picked up his book again.

More seagulls came.

They covered every inch of Wart.

“Vacation is vacation,”

said Wizard,

“but enough is enough!”

Wizard hopped and bopped.

"Fish eyes and icky stuff!"

he yelled.

Poof!

A goat stood

where each seagull had been.

"Sorry," Wizard told Wart.

"I should never do magic

in a hurry."

"I don't think they allow

goats at the beach," said Wart.

Chapter Two

There were goats
all over the beach.

Everybody sat in boats
on the sea.

"This is the life,"
Wizard said.
Wart ate cookies
and got seasick.

"Do magic," Wart begged.

"Get the goats off the beach

so we can go back there."

"I don't work on vacation,"

said Wizard.

Soon a flock of seagulls landed on Wart.

"Help!" cried Wart.

"A curse and worse!" yelled Wizard.

"Can't a wizard get a little rest?"

Wizard stomped and stormed.

"Seashells and whale tails!"

he shouted.

Splash!

Wizard fell into the sea.

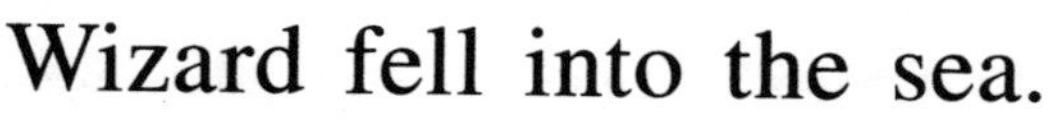

“Whales?” yelled Wart.
“Why did you change them
into whales?”
“It seemed like a good idea
at the time,”
said Wizard, and sneezed.

Chapter Three

The beach was full of goats.

The sea was full of whales.

Everybody crowded
around the hotel pool.

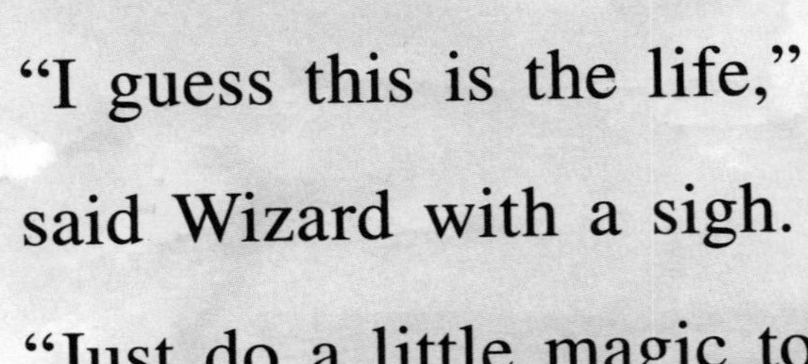

"I guess this is the life,"
said Wizard with a sigh.
"Just do a little magic to get rid
of the goats," said Wart.
"Then we can go to the beach."

"No more magic!" said Wizard.

"I don't work on vacation."

Soon a herd of seagulls
landed on Wart.
“Wait!” Wart shouted at Wizard,
but it was too late.
Wizard was already
fussing and fuming.

"Bat wings and monkey swings!"

he shouted.

Poof!

Then there were monkeys

where seagulls had been.

“You are rotten guests!”
the hotel clerk yelled.
“It is bad manners
to throw magic spells around.”

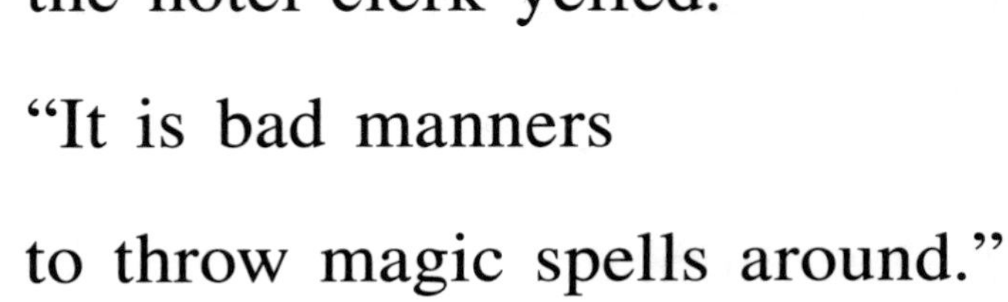

"No one can go on the beach
because of the goats,"
said the plumbers.
"No one can go in the sea
because of the whales,"
said the pansy potters.
"Now no one can swim in the pool
because of the monkeys!"
said the pickle packers.

"My goodness!" said Wizard.

"You all look terrible.

You need a vacation."

"Do something!"

yelled the hotel clerk.

Chapter Four

"Vacation's over," Wizard said.

"Make room for magic!"

Wizard razzled and dazzled.

"Oh!" said the guests. "Ah!"

"Good grief," said Wart.

"We can't go wrong
with birds of song," sang Wizard.
Poof!

The whales, goats, and monkeys
were gone.
Songbirds filled the sky.

"This is wonderful!"

said the potters, packers,

and plumbers.

"Come back anytime,"

said the hotel clerk.

Then he remembered

the goats.

"On second thought,

just keep in touch."

Then he remembered

the whales and monkeys.

"On last thought, just go away."

"It is time to go home," said Wizard.

"I am tired of sand, sea, and sun."

Wizard hopped and bopped.

Poof!

At home

Wizard settled down with his book.

Wart had a snack,

and soon he was snoring.

"This is the life," said Wizard.

And then he was snoring too.